SPOOKY SHADOWS

That night Joe tossed and turned in his sleeping bag. The ground was too hard. The air was too chilly. And outside, strange creatures made hissing and howling noises.

"*Psssst!* Frank!" Joe whispered. "Are you awake?"

No reply.

"*Bro!*" Joe said more loudly. "Are . . . you . . . awake?"

Frank snored and rolled over in his sleeping bag.

The moon lit up the walls of the tent and cast long, eerie shadows onto the boys. Joe eyed the shadows nervously. *They're just trees,* he told himself.

Then one of the shadows moved to the right. Footsteps crunched on the ground.

Someone—or *something*—was out there!

THE HARDY BOYS®

SECRET FILES #16

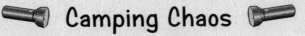 Camping Chaos

BY FRANKLIN W. DIXON

ILLUSTRATED BY SCOTT BURROUGHS

ALADDIN · NEW YORK LONDON TORONTO SYDNEY NEW DELHI

ALADDIN

An imprint of Simon & Schuster Children's Publishing Division
1230 Avenue of the Americas, New York, NY 10020
First Aladdin paperback edition December 2014
Text copyright © 2014 by Simon & Schuster, Inc.
Illustrations copyright © 2014 by Scott Burroughs
Series design by Lisa Vega
Cover design by Karina Granda
All rights reserved, including the right of reproduction in whole or in part in any form.
ALADDIN is a trademark of Simon & Schuster, Inc., and related logo is a registered trademark of Simon & Schuster, Inc.
THE HARDY BOYS is a registered trademark of Simon & Schuster, Inc.
For information about special discounts for bulk purchases, please contact Simon & Schuster Special Sales at 1-866-506-1949 or business@simonandschuster.com.
The Simon & Schuster Speakers Bureau can bring authors to your live event. For more information or to book an event contact the Simon & Schuster Speakers Bureau at 1-866-248-3049 or visit our website at www.simonspeakers.com.
The text of this book was set in Garamond.
Manufactured in the United States of America 1014 OFF
10 9 8 7 6 5 4 3 2 1
Library of Congress Control Number 2014949902
ISBN 978-1-4424-9048-2 (pbk)
ISBN 978-1-4424-9050-5 (eBook)

CONTENTS

Camping Chaos

1

Going Camping

Dibs on this campsite!" Frank Hardy announced, setting his sleeping bag down.

"Hey, don't I get a say? We're sharing a tent, remember?" his brother, Joe, reminded him.

"Trust me. This is the perfect spot," Frank insisted.

"Why?" Joe asked curiously.

"It faces the east, so the morning sun will warm us up. And there's lots of moss and leaves, so it'll be comfortable to sleep on," Frank replied.

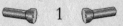

"Uh-huh. When did you turn into Mr. Camping Expert?" Joe teased him.

Frank grinned. "I read all about it in my camping book. Chapter two, 'Picking the Ideal Campsite.'"

Their friend Phil Cohen set his own sleeping bag down about ten feet away. "Yeah, well, Chet and I picked an even *better* spot. We used the new camping app on my cell phone." Phil loved apps, which were like computer programs. He had been obsessed with electronics since he was in first grade.

"What's so great about *your* spot?" Joe asked Phil.

"Well, the ground here slants a little. So if it rains, the water will wash downhill and not form a puddle under our tent," Phil explained. "Plus, we have a clear three-hundred-and-sixty-degree view all around us, so we can see any bears or panthers or other predators coming."

Chet Morton blinked at Phil. "B-bears? And p-panthers?" he stammered. "Um, maybe we should turn around and go home. . . ."

"Don't worry, Chet. There are no bears or panthers in Bayport State Park," Fenton Hardy said quickly. He glanced at his watch. "Come on. Let's get busy with our tents. It's almost time for the welcome meeting over at the main lodge."

Mr. Hardy was Frank and Joe's dad. He had brought the four boys to Bayport State Park for

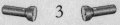

the annual fall Fun with Camping weekend. There would be hiking, canoeing, animal tracking, a tent-decorating contest, and other cool activities.

Frank pulled his camping book out of his backpack. He opened it to chapter 3, "How to Pitch Your Tent." He and Joe had pitched tents before, but it was good to get a refresher.

The brothers worked efficiently. First they cleared the ground of any rocks and branches that might dig into their backs while they slept. Next they laid down a tarp and smoothed it out with their hands. The tarp was waterproof and would prevent rain and other moisture from seeping in.

After that they inserted metal rods into their tent and popped it up. They set the structure upright on top of the tarp and staked it into the ground using a wooden mallet. Finally, they arranged their sleeping bags, lanterns, flashlights, and other equipment inside.

When they were done, Frank stepped back to admire their work. It was a perfect home away from home—for the next two nights, anyway!

Their dad finished pitching his tent on the other side of Frank and Joe's. Phil and Chet finished pitching their tent too. Then the five of them grabbed their water bottles and set off for the welcome meeting.

They took a narrow dirt path that meandered through the sun-dappled forest. The leaves on the trees blazed red, gold, and orange. Squirrels scurried around, busily collecting acorns. The air was cool and crisp and smelled like apples. Phil took lots of pictures with his camera phone along the way.

At the end of the path, they came to a wide clearing. In the middle of the clearing was a large log cabin with a sign that said: GOOSEBERRY LODGE.

Just outside the lodge, a bunch of kids and their parents sat on tree stumps arranged in a wide circle.

Frank recognized Beatrice Lesser and Lina Kim, who were in the fifth grade at Bayport Elementary School. Frank, Phil, and Chet were nine years old and in the fourth grade; Joe was eight and in the third grade.

The four boys and Mr. Hardy sat down on a row of tree stumps right behind Beatrice and Lina and their parents. Everyone was buzzing excitedly about the weekend. Beatrice and Lina were talking about their matching bright pink tents. A moment later a tall, lanky man in a gray-green ranger's uniform came into the center of the circle.

"Hello, everyone! I'm Ranger Gil," he said in a friendly voice. "I'm glad to see so many of you here for our fall Fun with Camping event. We have lots of great activities lined up for you. But first I want to introduce you to my counselors. They're both freshmen at Bayport College. Please give it up for Fish and Wendy!"

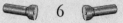

Everyone clapped as two older teens stood up and waved. The guy, Fish, was really tall and had spiky brown hair and chunky black glasses. The girl, Wendy, was really short and wore a navy-blue bandana over her messy red curls.

"I've never met anyone named Fish," Frank whispered to Joe.

"Maybe his favorite food is fish sticks," Joe joked.

Ranger Gil proceeded to go through a long list of important camping rules. They included never using soap in or near streams or ponds and building fires only in existing fireplaces and pits.

Then he described their schedule for the weekend. "Tonight we'll have a cookout here at Gooseberry Lodge, followed by our Friday Frightfest movie," he began. "Tomorrow there's animal tracking, and Sunday there's canoeing on Loon Lake. And of course, there's our big tent-decorating contest!"

"Did you remember to pack our decorations?" Frank asked Joe in a low voice.

Joe nodded. "Yup. In my duffel bag."

Beatrice turned around. "You guys shouldn't even bother. I'm totally going to win that contest!" she bragged.

2

The Invasion of
the Swamp Monsters

xcuse me?" Joe snapped. He glared at
Beatrice.

Joe didn't know Beatrice really well,
since she was two grades ahead in school. But
he'd heard from some of the other kids at Bayport
Elementary that she could be a big show-off.

"Yeah, my tent's going to be amazing," Beatrice said with a smirk. "It's going to have a princess theme!"

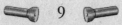

"Well, *ours* is going to be even better," Joe shot back. "Our theme is—"

"Shhh. Let's let Ranger Gil finish talking," Mr. Hardy whispered, putting his finger to his lips.

". . . you're all welcome to start decorating your tents before dinner. The deadline for finishing is tomorrow by lunch, and the winner will be announced on Sunday," Ranger Gil was saying. "So! I'll see you all back here at five for the cookout. That will be followed by a special screening of *The Invasion of the Swamp Monsters* inside the lodge."

Chet pumped his fist in the air. "*Yes!* I love that movie. I've seen it five times, and I have all the comic books, too."

"Big deal. I've seen it ten times. And comic books are for babies," Beatrice said, flipping her long blond hair over her shoulders.

Chet gave Beatrice a look as though she were

 10

crazy. He was a *huge* comic book fan, and so were Phil and the Hardys.

"Is Beatrice obnoxious, or what?" Joe muttered to Frank.

"Just ignore her," Frank advised.

As soon as the welcome meeting was over, Joe and his group started back in the direction of their campsites. As they passed the two counselors, Fish and Wendy, Joe heard Fish say: "So this is your first job as a counselor, huh?"

"Yeah. Got any advice for me?" Wendy asked him.

"Just make it superfun for the kids," Fish replied.

Sounds perfect, Joe thought. He just hoped that certain campers, like ones named Beatrice, didn't spoil the fun for everyone else.

Joe had actually never seen *The Invasion of the Swamp Monsters* before. As he, Frank, Chet, and Phil

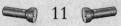

huddled together in the darkened lodge snacking on sodas and nacho-cheese-flavored popcorn, Joe found himself more scared than he'd thought he would be. He was secretly glad that his dad was sitting close by, although he would never admit that to anyone.

All the campers and their parents were in what was called the "great room" of the lodge. At one end of the great room was an enormous stone fireplace. At the other end was a large plasma-screen TV. Maps of the region covered the walls, along with posters about insects, birds, and rocks. There was

a glass case filled with snake skins, different kinds of fossils, and a stuffed fox with beady golden eyes.

Joe liked the great room. He especially liked the snake skins, since he and Frank planned on a snake theme for the tent-decorating contest. In fact, they'd already started decorating before dinner, draping toy snakes over the top of their tent.

And speaking of slithery, slimy creatures . . .

A swamp monster appeared on the TV screen. It staggered across the marsh with its dripping wet arms outstretched, ready to attack. Joe grabbed a handful of popcorn and munched intently.

Just then he felt icy-cold fingers on the back of his neck.

"Agggghhh!" he yelled.

The lights snapped on. Joe spun around. A little boy with short, curly brown hair and freckles grinned at him. He was holding a soda can.

Joe's cheeks grew hot. So *that* was what had grazed

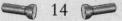 14

the back of his neck. How embarrassing was that?

Ranger Gil hit the pause button on the movie. "What on earth is going on?" he demanded.

"Did my ginger ale scare you?" the boy asked Joe with a giggle.

"Garrett! Come over here right this second," Ranger Gil ordered.

"But, Daddy, it's not my fault! My soda can touched him!" Garrett insisted.

"Over here, *now*!" Ranger Gil repeated sternly.

"Oh, okay." Garrett stood up and shuffled over to his father with a glum expression.

"Are you all right?" Mr. Hardy asked Joe.

"Yeah. I just feel dumb," Joe mumbled.

After a moment Garrett returned to his seat. "My daddy says I'm supposed to tell you I'm sorry," he said with a shrug.

"Apology accepted. Just don't do that again, okay?" Joe told him.

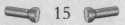

"But this movie's so *boooring*," Garrett complained.

"What? This is, like, the best movie ever! Wait till we get to the part where the swamp monster takes over New York City!" Chet spoke up.

Ranger Gil turned the lights off and resumed the movie. Joe scooted over so he sat farther away from Garrett. The ranger's son seemed like trouble. Hopefully, he wouldn't bother Joe again over the weekend.

That night Joe tossed and turned in his sleeping bag. The ground was too hard. The air was too chilly. And outside, strange creatures made hissing and howling noises.

"*Psssst!* Frank!" Joe whispered. "Are you awake?"

No reply.

"*Bro!*" Joe said more loudly. "Are . . . you . . . awake?"

Frank snored and rolled over in his sleeping bag.

The moon lit up the walls of the tent and cast long, eerie shadows onto the boys. Joe eyed the shadows nervously. *They're just trees,* he told himself.

Then one of the shadows moved to the right. Footsteps crunched on the ground.

Someone—or *something*—was out there!

3

Mysterious Footprints

"Frank! Wake *up*!" Joe reached over and shook his brother, hard.

"What?" Frank mumbled groggily, rubbing his eyes. "I was having the best dream ever. We were at the arcade, and I scored a million points on Space Raiders, and—"

"Forget about that. There's a person outside our tent. Or maybe it's a wild animal!" Joe whispered.

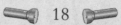

Frank sat up. "Wait, what? How do you know?" he whispered back.

"Listen!"

Frank listened. He could hear an owl hooting in the distance. He could also hear Chet muttering in his sleep—something about bears and panthers. Or was it brownies and pizza?

"There's nobody out there," Frank told Joe after a moment.

"There is! You should go outside and take a look," Joe suggested.

"Why don't *you* take a look?"

"Fine! Let's *both* go."

The brothers scooted up to the front of the tent and peeked through the flaps. Moonlight spilled onto the landscape and illuminated tents, trees, rocks—but nothing else.

"See?" Frank hissed.

 19

"I *know* I heard someone," Joe insisted. "What if it was the swamp monster?"

Frank rolled his eyes at Joe and went back to bed.

The next morning Frank woke up early. He pulled his Bayport Bandits hoodie on over his pajamas, stepped into the sunshine, and stretched. It was going to be a beautiful day.

He was glad they were spending the weekend at the park. Camping was really awesome!

Except for the part when your little brother wakes you up in the middle of the night because he's imagining things, he thought, shaking his head.

Mr. Hardy, Phil, and Chet were apparently still asleep, as was Joe. Frank decided to make a fire so he could heat up water for hot chocolate. His mom had packed the kind he liked, with the little marshmallows that floated on top. He remembered Ranger Gil's rule about building fires only in existing fireplaces and pits.

Frank started for the edge of the forest to collect some wood. Through the trees, he could make out a bunch of other tents in the distance, including two matching bright pink tents. *Must be Beatrice's and Lina's,* he thought.

Then Frank stopped. There was something on the ground near his and Joe's tent.

Footprints.

He bent down and inspected them closely. They were about the same size as his and Joe's shoes. But the sole had an unfamiliar pattern. It was a zigzag design, like a lightning bolt.

Who was hanging around our tent last night—and why? Frank wondered. He saw that the footprints looped in a big circle from the main path, to their tent, and back again.

Phil and Chet had left their sneakers just outside their tent. Frank picked them up and studied the soles. *No lightning-bolt pattern.*

Joe poked his head out of the Hardy boys' tent.

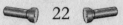 22

"Why are you up at the crack of dawn?" he called out sleepily.

"It's not dawn, lazy. It's almost seven thirty. Hey, check this out," Frank said, pointing.

Joe stepped out of the tent. Frank showed him the footprints.

"I *told* you!" Joe exclaimed. "The question is, Who—"

"What, When, Where, Why, and How?" Frank finished.

The Hardys were detectives, and they'd solved a lot of mysteries—everything from a zombie sighting to a missing dinosaur fossil. For every case, they wrote down Who, What, When, Where, Why, and How on a whiteboard in the secret tree house that their dad had built for them in their backyard at home.

Whenever they had a new theory, clue, or other information, they wrote it on the whiteboard under one of the six categories. They'd nicknamed their note-taking method the "six *W*s," even though "How" was not technically a *W* word.

Joe circled their tent once, then twice. He stopped in his tracks and frowned.

"I just figured out the Why," he announced. "Somebody stole our snake decorations in the middle of the night!"

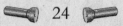

"*What?*"

Frank scanned the outside of their tent. The night before, he and Joe had decorated it with a bunch of snakes—plastic ones, rubber ones, and even some plush ones too. They'd found them in their attic at home, in a cardboard box labeled OLD TOYS.

"What are you talking about, Joe? They're right here!" Frank said.

"Not all of them," Joe corrected. "Perry the Python is missing. So are Bob the Boa Constrictor and Andy the Anaconda."

Frank did a double take. "Huh. You're right."

"So now we have our What, When, and Where," Joe noted. "What—stealing snakes. When—between Friday bedtime and Saturday morning. Where—right underneath our noses!"

"It looks like we have a new case on our hands," Frank said grimly.

 25

4

The Return of the Thief

A short while later everyone gathered outside Gooseberry Lodge for breakfast. Ranger Gil made pancakes and bacon on the grill while the counselors, Fish and Wendy, passed out cups of apple cider.

Joe noticed Beatrice and Lina huddled together and whispering. At one point Beatrice glanced over her shoulder at Joe and said something to Lina. Then the two of them got up and took off.

Were they talking about me? Joe wondered.

 26

He piled a plate high with pancakes and sat down on a tree stump next to Frank. "I don't like fifth-grade girls," he muttered.

"Never mind that. I have an idea about how we can solve this case," Frank said in a low voice.

Joe folded a pancake in half and stuffed the whole thing into his mouth. Maple syrup dribbled down his chin; he wiped it off with the back of his sleeve. "How?" he mumbled with his mouth half-full.

"You know that bank robbery case Dad worked on?"

Joe frowned, trying to remember. He wasn't sure which bank robbery case Frank was talking about. Their father was a private investigator who'd consulted with the Bayport Police on dozens of cases. Before that he'd been a member of the NYPD—the New York Police Department.

"Remind me," Joe said, picking up another pancake.

"Last summer Dad solved a bank robbery case. His only clue was the footprint the robber left behind at the Bayport National Bank," Frank said. "There was a funny pattern on the sole, like crisscrossed arrows. It turned out only one store in town carried that kind of shoe. And the store owner remembered selling a pair to the robber. He gave Dad a description of the robber and a copy of the receipt and everything."

Joe nodded. "Oh, yeah! That was awesome!"

"We can do the same thing here. If we can inspect the bottoms of everyone's shoes, we might be able to find the lightning-bolt pattern," Frank explained.

Joe considered this. "Yeah, but how? We can't just go around asking people if we can check out their shoes!"

"Yeah, we can. I have a plan. Follow me!"

Frank stood up and started walking up to the other campers one by one. Joe followed. With each camper, Frank explained that he had lost his super-valuable lucky coin somewhere in the vicinity, and that he and Joe needed to search the ground underneath the campers' feet.

The plan actually worked. Each camper lifted his or her feet so the Hardys could look for the "lucky coin"—and at the same time secretly examine the soles of everyone's shoes.

None of them had the lightning-bolt pattern, however. And Beatrice and Lina had left breakfast early, so the boys hadn't been able to see their shoes.

"Now what?" Joe asked Frank as they returned to their tree stumps.

Just then Ranger Gil's son, Garrett, strolled by, flipping through a pile of superhero cards. He wore a fleece jacket that was several sizes too big for him over his dinosaur pajamas.

Hmm, Joe thought. Garrett had pranked Joe at the movie the night before with the ice-cold soda can. Could he have pulled a second prank by stealing the snakes?

"Hey, Garrett!" Joe called out.

Garrett turned. "Oh! Hi!"

"Hi! Listen, did you come by our tent last night? Say, around midnight?" Joe asked him with a friendly smile.

Garrett scrunched up his face. "No way! My bedtime's eight o'clock. Which is *waaaay* too early, because I'm six now—almost six and a quarter!"

"Wow, six and a quarter!" Joe exclaimed. He looked down at Garrett's sneakers. They were green with orange stripes. "Hey, I like your shoes! Are they that new kind with the really cool design on the soles?"

"What?" Garrett lifted his shoes. The soles had a polka-dot pattern.

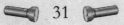

Frank and Joe exchanged a glance. No lightning bolt.

Garrett waved good-bye and wandered over to the pancake station. The Hardys finished their food in silence. They had to come up with another plan if they were going to get Perry the Python, Bob the Boa Constrictor, and Andy the Anaconda back. After all, the deadline for decorating their tent was lunchtime. Besides, Perry, Bob, and Andy belonged to *them*.

• • • •

After breakfast Joe and Frank headed back to their campsite along with Phil and Chet. Mr. Hardy stayed at the lodge to help Ranger Gil and the counselors with cleanup.

Phil held up his cell phone. "My compass app says that our tents are this way," he said, pointing at a trailhead.

"Uh, thanks, Phil. We'd all be totally lost without your app," Joe joked.

"What will you do if you don't find your missing snakes?" Chet asked the Hardys.

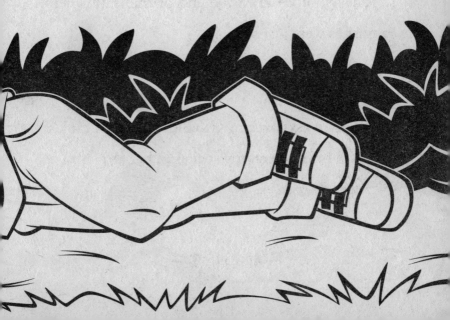

"We'll find them," Frank replied. But he didn't look so sure.

"Phil and I could let you borrow some of our decorations, but our space alien theme doesn't really go with your snake theme," Chet offered. "Unless you want to do a killer-snakes-from-outer-space theme. That could work!"

Joe dropped down onto the ground and pretended to slither on his stomach. "Take . . . me . . . to . . . your . . . leader! *Sssssss!*" he hissed.

The other boys cracked up.

They soon reached the end of the trail. Their campsites were just ahead.

As they got closer to the campsite, Joe noticed something strange.

A girl was hovering around his and Frank's tent. She held several toy snakes in her arms.

The snake thief!

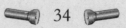 34

5

The Six *W*s

"T here's our thief!" Joe yelled out to Frank.

The two boys took off running. Phil and Chet followed.

When they got closer to the tent, they could see that the girl had long black hair and glasses. *Lina!*

"Hey! Put those snakes back right now!" Frank shouted.

Lina whirled around, clutching the snakes to her chest. "That's what I'm doing. Why are you yelling at me?"

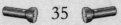

"What do you mean, that's what you're doing?" Joe demanded.

"I'm putting your snakes back," Lina explained.

Frank saw that she was holding a toy python, boa constrictor, and anaconda. "Hey, that's Perry, Bob, and Andy. Where did you get them?"

Joe's eyes widened. "Oh, *now* I get it! She stole them last night. And she's trying to sneak them back so she won't get into trouble."

"I didn't steal them!" Lina protested. "I found

them near my tent. I went around to all the camp-sites to see who they belonged to. I just got here."

She handed the snakes to Frank. He took them from her.

Frank tried to read Lina's expression. She wouldn't look him in the eye. Did that mean she was lying?

"I'm missing some decorations from my tent too, and so is Beatrice," Lina continued. "Someone stole them from our tents last night. We thought it was you guys."

"What?" Joe gasped. "You think *we're* the thieves?"

"What kind of decorations are you and Beatrice missing?" Phil asked Lina curiously.

"Beatrice is missing her doll, Princess Petunia. She's decorating her tent with a princess theme," Lina replied. "I'm missing my toy tiger, Mr. Truffles. I'm decorating my tent with a safari theme."

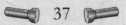 37

"Is anyone else missing decorations?" Frank asked.

Lina shrugged. "I don't know. Anyway, I'm glad I found your snakes. I just hope someone finds Mr. Truffles soon—and Princess Petunia, too."

Inside their tent Frank dug through his backpack. He pulled out his camping book, a pair of socks, some comic books, and a Space Raiders T-shirt and dumped them onto his sleeping bag. The socks were kind of smelly; he wadded them up and tossed them into the corner.

"What are you looking for?" Joe asked.

"These!" Frank pulled out an old notebook and a stubby pencil with no eraser, and showed them to Joe. "We can use these for our six *W*s, since we don't have our whiteboard here."

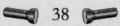

He opened the notebook to a clean page and wrote:

WHO

WHAT

WHEN

WHERE

WHY

HOW

Next to the What, Frank wrote:

Someone stole three of our snakes and put them over by Lina's tent. The same person (?) stole her toy tiger, Mr. Truffles, and Beatrice's Princess Petunia doll. They're still missing.

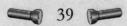

Next to the When, he added:

Sometime between Friday bedtime
and Saturday morning.

Finally, he wrote next to the Where:

At our campsite and Lina's and
Beatrice's campsites.

Joe read the notes over Frank's shoulder. "Now we just need to figure out the Who, Why, and How," Joe murmured. "Any ideas about the Who?"

Frank mulled this over. "Lina could be lying. Maybe she pretended Mr. Truffles is missing, as a cover-up," he said after a moment.

"Or it could be Beatrice," Joe suggested.

"Or Beatrice and Lina together. They're, like, best friends," Frank pointed out.

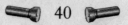 40

"And don't forget about Ranger Gil's son, Garrett! He's a troublemaker," Joe added.

"Yeah, but his shoes didn't have the lightning-bolt pattern," Frank reminded him.

Joe considered this. "Maybe he was wearing different shoes last night."

Frank nodded. "Hmm, true."

Next to the Who, Frank added:

Lina?
Beatrice?
Garrett?

At this point they had more questions than answers.

That afternoon Fish and Wendy led the campers on an animal-tracking expedition through the forest. Animal tracking involved finding tracks, or

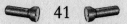

prints, on the ground and identifying what animal they belonged to.

Ranger Gil wasn't there. He was back at Gooseberry Lodge with Garrett, who was in a time-out because he'd smeared pancake batter all over the lodge windows.

Joe's right. Garrett is definitely a troublemaker! Frank thought.

"Being a good animal tracker is like being a detective," Fish explained as the group hiked along a winding creek. "You have to ask yourselves a lot of 'what,' 'where,' 'when,' 'how,' and 'why' questions to get to the 'who.'"

Frank and Joe grinned at each other. That sounded just like the six *W*s!

"First step: Look for tracks on the ground. Then ask yourself, how many toes does the animal have?" Fish said.

"I see a track! I see a track!" a camper said,

jumping up and down excitedly. "It has two toes!"

Fish nodded and gave a thumbs-up sign. "Good, Zack! Two toes means that it could be a deer or a moose—"

"Or a deadly two-toed flesh-eating swamp monster," Wendy cut in with a mischievous smile.

Several campers shrieked.

"Wendy's kidding," Fish said quickly, then turned to her. *"Really?"* he asked her in a low voice.

Wendy shrugged. "Just trying to keep it fun, dude."

"Okay, well . . . back to our animal-tracking questions," Fish went on, pushing his glasses up his nose. "Ask yourselves, are the tracks spaced far apart? That will tell you if the animal is big or small, and how fast it was going. Also, do the tracks have claw marks? Do they stop at a tree, which would tell you that the animal is able to climb?"

 43

He added, "If there was snow on the ground, we'd be able to figure out a lot more. For example, did you know that you can sometimes identify a fox by the trail of yellow pee that it leaves behind?"

"*Ewwww!*" some of the campers groaned. Others cracked up.

"Ohmigosh!" Beatrice cried out suddenly.

"Did you find a track, Beatrice?" Fish asked her.

Beatrice shook her head and pointed to a large boulder in the middle of the creek. "No, but I found something else. There's Princess Petunia!" she exclaimed. "Somebody save her!"

6

The Legend of
the Headless Ghost

J oe stared. A doll was perched on a rock in the middle of the creek. She wore a sparkly gold crown on top of her long blond hair, and a fancy purple dress.

How did Princess Petunia end up there? Joe wondered.

"I'll get her!" Wendy volunteered.

She pulled off her pink hiking shoes and rolled her jeans up to her knees. She stepped into the

water and waded out to the boulder. "Brrr, it's cold!" she said with a laugh.

"This is epic," Phil murmured. "Camp counselor rescues missing doll in the middle of a raging river!" He pulled out his camera phone and snapped a couple of pictures.

Wendy emerged from the creek and handed Beatrice her doll. "Thank you!" Beatrice said happily. "Princess Petunia, you're back!"

On an impulse Joe headed over to the bank of the creek. As he passed a bush, a deer burst out and bounded away, startling him.

He bent down and inspected the ground. There was a jumble of different footprints—*human* footprints.

There were several footprints with a lightning-bolt pattern!

"Hey, what's up?" Phil asked, joining Joe.

Joe nodded at the footprints. "We think these belong to the person who's been stealing stuff," he explained.

Phil aimed his camera phone at the footprints and took a picture.

"Joe! Phil! We need to keep moving," Fish called out. "Did you guys find an interesting animal track?"

"I guess you could say that," Joe replied with a sly smile.

Later that night everyone met at Gooseberry Lodge for make-your-own tacos, followed by ghost stories and roasted marshmallows around a roaring bonfire.

After dinner Joe and Frank grabbed a couple of long sticks and a bag of marshmallows and sat down on a log. The evening was especially chilly, so the warmth of the fire was welcome.

 48

Joe speared a marshmallow with his stick and thrust it into the fire. It immediately sizzled and burst into flames.

"Whoa!" Joe frowned at the blackened blob at the end of his stick. "Marshmallow fail!"

"You have to be patient, Bro. Hold it away from the fire a bit," Frank suggested.

Joe sighed and tried again with a new marshmallow. As he waited for it to cook, he thought about their case.

So far he, Frank, Beatrice, and Lina seemed to be the only victims of the thief. At dinner the Hardy boys had gone around and asked the other campers if they were missing any decorations, and they'd all said no.

Perry, Bob, and Andy had been found, as had Beatrice's Princess Petunia doll. But Lina's toy tiger, Mr. Truffles, was still missing.

The footprint with the lightning bolt was their only clue so far, and they'd seen it twice— once this morning at their tent, and once this afternoon by the creek. Joe and Frank had managed to check out the bottoms of Beatrice's and Lina's shoes at dinner, using the same lucky-coin story they'd used that morning. Neither had the lightning-bolt pattern. Although maybe the girls had brought more than one pair of shoes for the weekend?

Joe frowned. He felt as though they were miss-

ing something important. Maybe it was the Why part of the equation. Why would the thief do all this? Was he or she trying to win the tent-decorating contest? If so, that would point to Beatrice, who'd bragged to Joe the day before that she would definitely win. She could have *pretended* to steal her own doll—and Lina's tiger, Mr. Truffles, too—just to confuse everyone.

Or was the thief simply trying to make trouble? That would point to Garrett, who seemed like a Troublemaker with a capital *T*—first with the soda can incident last night, and then with the pancake batter incident this morning.

Or did the thief have another motive altogether? Was it someone Joe and Frank hadn't even thought of?

A hush fell over the group as Ranger Gil leaned closer to the bonfire and began telling a scary story. "According to an old legend these woods

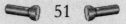 51

are haunted by a headless ghost," he said in a low, spooky voice.

"A headless ghost? *Cooool!*" Garrett piped up eagerly.

"Don't interrupt, Garrett. Anyway, legend has it that the ghost wanders around the park in search of his missing head. No one knows how he lost it. But many people have reported seeing him, especially when there's a full moon. . . ."

Joe glanced up at the sky—and gulped.

There was a full moon tonight.

Joe tossed and turned that night, unable to fall sleep. *Again.* He missed his and Frank's bunk bed back home. He missed being in a warm, cozy house. He missed his mom's cooking. He even missed Aunt Gertrude, who lived with them, nagging at him and Frank to clean up their room.

And he definitely missed not having to worry about headless ghosts.

It's just a dumb made-up story, he told himself over and over again. Still, he wished there weren't a full moon tonight.

He had almost fallen asleep when he heard a scream outside.

It sounded like Chet!

7

A Spy in the Bushes

Frank bolted up in his sleeping bag at the sound of the scream. For a second he didn't know where he was. "Where are we? What's happening?" he demanded.

"Someone's in trouble. I think it might be Chet!" Joe said, scrambling to his feet.

"*Oh!*"

Frank grabbed a flashlight, and the two boys rushed outside in their pajamas and socks. Mr. Hardy was already outside with his own flashlight.

Miniature glow-in-the-dark UFOs and martians shone eerily on Phil and Chet's tent.

"Everything's fine," Mr. Hardy told Frank and Joe immediately. "I think our poor Chet had a nightmare."

"But it *wasn't* a nightmare, Mr. Hardy," Chet said, pulling a hoodie over his T-shirt and sweatpants. "I heard a noise outside, and I peeked out. I saw a headless ghost! I swear it!"

"It could have been an animal," Frank suggested.

Chet shook his head. "No way. It was definitely a ghost!"

"Did you see it too?" Joe asked Phil.

"Nope. I was fast asleep—until Chet started yelling, anyway," Phil replied, zipping up his parka.

"What did this ghost look like?" Frank asked Chet.

Chet shuddered. "It was white and superscary. You know, like a ghost! And it was moving around!"

Frank waved his flashlight around. Leaves stirred, and a small animal skittered away.

And then Frank noticed something on the ground—something white. He walked over and pointed his flashlight at it.

"Here's your ghost, Chet," Frank announced, holding up a blanket. "I think you got pranked."

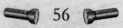

The next morning Frank, Joe, Phil, and Chet built a campfire in the fire pit by their tents and drank hot chocolate with little marshmallows in it while Mr. Hardy went for a jog. They inspected the blanket they'd found the night before.

There was a label sewn onto one corner of the fabric. It had three letters on it: *HOF*.

"What's 'HOF'?" Chet asked. He pronounced it like "hof."

"Maybe it's the name of the company that made the blanket?" Phil guessed.

Joe pointed to the letters. "They're written in Magic Marker. So maybe they're initials?"

"Like the initials of the person who owns the blanket," Frank spoke up. "Aunt Gertrude some- times sews labels onto our clothes. She writes our initials on them."

"Yes!" Joe said eagerly. "Now all we have to do is figure out which camper has the initials *H-O-F.*"

The boys mulled this over. "Let's make a list of everyone who's here for the weekend," Frank sug- gested. "Okay, so there's the four of us, Beatrice, and Lina . . ."

"And there's Zack and Zack's sister, whose

name begins with a *C.* . . . I can't remember what it is. . . . Oh, and don't forget about my buddy Garrett," Joe added.

"Zack's sister's name is Caitlin. Plus there's those five kids from Hudson Falls. I think their names are Grey, Liam, Ethan, Padma, and Dev," Chet went on.

"So, no *H*s," Phil concluded.

They sat in silence for a long moment.

"Maybe the blanket belongs to one of the parents," Frank said finally.

"You think a parent decided to pull a prank and pretend to be a ghost? That doesn't make any sense," Joe replied.

Just then Frank heard a twig snap. He glanced up sharply. Was it an animal—or a person?

"What's that noise?" Joe whispered.

"Maybe it's a bear or a panther," Chet replied nervously. "We should hide!"

 59

Bushes rustled. As the boys looked over, they caught a glimpse of dark brown hair disappearing back behind the bushes.

Frank and Joe glanced at each other. Someone was spying on them!

8

A Surprise Suspect

"ho's there?" Joe called out.

There was no reply.

Joe put his finger to his lips, signaling to Frank, Chet, and Phil that they should be quiet. He moved quickly in the direction of the bushes, trying to make as little noise as possible.

When he got there, he leaped forward and grabbed a handful of leaves—and then a mass of dark brown curls.

"*Ow!*" a voice cried out.

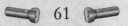

"Come out of there, whoever you are," Joe ordered.

A moment later Garrett stepped out, his cheeks flushed red. He clutched a stuffed animal to his chest and glared at Joe.

"You're *mean*!" he complained, rubbing his head. "I'm telling my daddy, and you are going to be in so much trouble!"

"Well, you're going to be in so much trouble

too," Joe snapped. "Didn't your daddy tell you that you shouldn't spy on people?"

Garrett pouted. "But I was so *boooored*! And you guys were talking about awesome stuff, like ghosts!"

Frank, Chet, and Phil joined them. Frank held up the white blanket. "Did you wear this last night and pretend to be a ghost?" he asked Garrett.

Garrett shook his head. "No way!"

Joe eyed Garrett's stuffed animal. It looked like a tiger!

"Where did you get that?" Joe demanded.

Garrett hugged the tiger protectively. "It's mine! I found it by the frog pond this morning! Finders, keepers!"

Joe reached over and peered at the tiger's collar. A rhinestone nametag read: MR. TRUFFLES.

"It's Lina's missing tiger!" he told Frank. "Mystery solved!"

"We haven't solved the mystery *yet*," Frank corrected Joe. "We still have to figure out who our thief is—and our ghost, too!"

"It's got to be Garrett," Joe said to Frank.

The two boys sat in their tent, updating their six *W*s. Phil and Chet had gone to the lodge for breakfast along with Mr. Hardy. Frank and Joe had promised to catch up to them.

Frank flipped to the page they'd started yesterday and filled in all their new information. He missed their whiteboard system back home. It was hard keeping up the six *W*s with only a paper and pencil!

> WHO: Lina?
> Beatrice?
> Garrett?
> A person with the initials HOF?

WHAT: Someone stole three of our snakes and put them over by Lina's tent. The same person (?) stole her toy tiger, Mr. Truffles, and Beatrice's Princess Petunia doll. ~~They're still missing.~~

Plus, the same person (?) wore a white blanket with the initials HOF and pretended to be a ghost.

WHEN: ~~Sometime between Friday bedtime and Saturday morning.~~ The snakes were stolen sometime between Friday bedtime and Saturday morning. They turned up on Saturday morning.

Princess Petunia and Mr. Truffles were stolen sometime between Friday bedtime and Saturday morning too.

 65

Princess Petunia turned up on Saturday afternoon, and Mr. Truffles turned up on Sunday morning.

The ghost thing happened Saturday night.

WHERE: ~~At our campsite and Lina's and Beatrice's campsites.~~ Our snakes were stolen from our tent and turned up near Lina's tent. Princess Petunia was stolen from Beatrice's tent and turned up on a rock in the middle of the creek. Mr. Truffles was stolen from Lina's tent, and Garrett found it by the frog pond.

The ghost thing happened by our campsite.

WHY: Maybe the person really wants to win the tent-decorating contest?

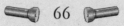 66

> *Or maybe the person just wants to make trouble?*
>
> *Or maybe it's just a bunch of stupid camp pranks?*

Joe leaned over and peered at Frank's notes. "I think our best bet is to figure out who the white blanket belongs to," he said after a moment. "Why don't we ask around and find out who has the initials *H-O-F*?"

"Actually, why don't we ask the one person who would *definitely* know?" Frank suggested.

The Hardys found Ranger Gil in Gooseberry Lodge, getting ready for the morning's canoeing expedition on Loon Lake.

"Hi, Ranger Gil. Do you know if any of the campers here have the initials *H-O-F*?" Joe asked him immediately.

"*H-O-F*? Hmm, doesn't sound familiar, but let me double-check the registration list," Ranger Gil offered.

The Hardys waited while Ranger Gil pulled his cell phone out of his pocket and scrolled through the screens. The phone had dinosaur stickers on it. "My son," Ranger Gil explained, pointing to the stickers. "Nope, we don't have any *H-O-F*s. Why do you ask?"

"We found a white blanket at our campsite, and the label has those initials. We're trying to find the owner," Frank explained.

"I can tell you that it's not mine or Garrett's. I have a green blanket, and his is blue," Ranger Gil said. "I know . . . why don't you put it in our lost-and-found box, which is in my office? I'll also let our counselors know to check with the other campers and their parents."

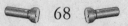

"Thanks, Ranger Gil," Joe said. He and Frank turned to go.

"Oh, boys? I just thought of someone," Ranger Gil said suddenly. "I don't know his middle name, but . . . anyway, it's Harold Fishbein."

Frank and Joe stopped in their tracks. "Who?" Frank asked, confused.

"Harold Fishbein. You know, Fish!" Ranger Gil said.

The Hardys stared at each other in surprise.

Was Fish their ghost—and also their thief?

9

The Clue in the Photograph

Loon Lake was as still as glass as the campers, parents, Ranger Gil, and Wendy set out in their canoes. A great blue heron sunned itself on a rock. Mountains loomed in the distance, bright with the colors of autumn.

Harold Fishbein, aka Fish, was nowhere in sight.

"Hey, Wendy. Where's Fish?" Frank called out from the canoe he and Joe shared.

Wendy shrugged. "Dunno, Hardys. He might

be resting in his tent. He said he was coming down with a cold."

Joe was about to say something to Frank. But Frank shook his head, cutting off his brother. Frank didn't want the two of them discussing the case while they were on the lake. Sound traveled easily over open water, which meant that other people might be able to hear them even if they whispered. In fact, Frank could make out Beatrice and Lina's conversation— about glittery versus non-glittery headbands—from practically halfway across Loon Lake.

As Frank drew the oars through the water, he thought about Fish. Fish was alone at the campground while everyone else was on the lake. Was he using the opportunity to steal more stuff? Or perform some other mischief?

Why was he doing all this?

Or was Fish actually sick? Maybe he wasn't the thief or ghost after all.

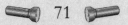 71

Forty-five minutes later, the group returned to shore. "Okay, gang! We'll meet at the lodge at noon for our farewell lunch. We'll be announcing the winners of our tent-decorating contest!" Ranger Gil told everyone.

Frank and Joe took off to find Fish while Phil, Chet, and Mr. Hardy headed back to their campsites. Frank had remembered to put the white blanket in his backpack.

Walking around, they saw some of the other campers' tent decorations. Frank's favorite was Zack's zombie-theme decorations. Joe's favorite was Zack's sister Caitlin's shark-theme decorations.

They finally found Fish in Gooseberry Lodge. He was in the kitchen, dressed in his pajamas and purple sneakers and gulping down a glass of orange juice.

"Hey, guys. I'm sick. You'd better stay away from me," Fish called out in a croaky-sounding

 72

voice. He blew his nose into a big white hand-kerchief.

Frank noticed that the handkerchief had ini-tials embroidered on it: *HOF.*

Yes! He and Joe were on the brink of cracking the case!

"So your real name is Harold Fishbein, huh? What's your middle name?" Frank asked Fish.

Fish blew his nose again. "Oliver. Why do you want to know?"

Frank pulled the white blanket out of his back-pack. "Is this yours?"

Fish blinked in surprise. "Yes! Thank you! I've been looking all over for it!"

"You . . . lost it?" Joe said, puzzled.

Fish nodded. "Yup. It went missing from my clothesline last night. That's probably why I got sick. It was freezing in the middle of the night!"

A door opened and shut. A moment later Phil

 73

and Chet came running into the kitchen.

"We've been looking all over for you guys," Phil said breathlessly. "We have something to show you!"

"Now? Because we're kind of busy," Joe said, nodding in Fish's direction.

"You're gonna want to see this," Chet piped up. *"In private."*

Joe glanced at Frank. Frank shrugged and nodded. The brothers said good-bye to Fish and followed Phil and Chet outside.

"Okay. What's so important?" Frank asked the two boys.

Phil pulled his cell phone out of his pocket and scrolled through the screens. "I was looking through my photos from this weekend," he began.

"So?" Joe said.

"So, remember this one?" Phil held up the phone for the Hardys to see.

On it was a picture of the lightning-bolt footprint.

"Yeah. You took that yesterday by the creek," Joe recalled.

"Do you remember what *else* I took yesterday by the creek?" Phil prodded.

 75

Joe and Frank shook their heads.

Phil touched the screen again. A different image came up.

It was a picture of a pair of pink hiking shoes lying in the weeds. In the background was Princess Petunia sitting on a rock in the middle of the creek.

Phil magnified the image and zoomed in on the bottoms of the shoes. Frank squinted at them. The soles had lightning bolts on them!

"I know who they belong to!" Frank said excitedly.

10

And the Winner Is . . .

Wendy!" Joe and Frank said in unison.

"You mean Wendy, our counselor?" Chet asked.

Frank nodded. "She waded into the creek to rescue Princess Petunia, remember? She took off her shoes before she went in!" He added, "I guess she has small feet. Her footprints were the same size as ours!"

Joe mulled all this over. They finally had their Who. But they still didn't have their Why.

"Okay, so why would Wendy steal our stuff? And pretend to be a ghost?" he asked Frank.

"There's only one way to find out," Frank replied.

The four boys headed over to Wendy's tent. Fortunately, she was there, packing up her gear.

"Hey, Hardy dudes and Phil and the Chetster!" she called out when she saw them. "Did you have an awesome weekend? Don't forget to tell all your friends so they'll come next year!"

"We know what you did, Wendy," Joe blurted out.

Wendy blinked. "Excuse me?"

Frank explained they had talked to Fish about the white blanket.

"Oh!" Wendy sighed heavily. "Okay, so I guess I've been busted. But I had a good reason to steal Fish's blanket! Well, *borrow*, technically."

"Did you have a good reason to 'borrow' our snakes, too? And Princess Petunia and Mr. Truffles?" Frank demanded.

 78

"Yes! I was just trying to make things fun!" Wendy explained.

"Fun?" Joe was totally confused.

Wendy nodded. "This is my first counseling job. Well, kind of my first job *ever*. Fish told me it was important that I make things superfun for you campers. So I tried to come up with some wild and crazy ideas. Like making stuff disappear and then reappear in the wrong places. And pretending to be a ghost."

She turned to Chet. "I wasn't expecting you to think I was a real ghost! You screamed so loudly that I just kind of ran. I feel bad about that. I guess I owe you an apology."

She added, "I guess I owe *all* of you an apology."

"Best . . . cupcakes . . . ever," Chet said as he scarfed down his third chocolate-chip-and-peanut-butter cupcake.

"I'm definitely coming back next fall," Phil agreed, stuffing a banana cupcake into his mouth.

Wendy had driven into town before lunch and picked up several dozen cupcakes at a bakery, to make up for what she'd done. The campers were enjoying them now for dessert as Ranger Gil announced the winners of the tent-decorating contest.

"Our third-place winner is Zack and his zombie tent!" Ranger Gil said. "Zack, come up and get your medal."

Everyone clapped as Zack rose to his feet and went up to claim his medal.

"Our second-place winner is Lina and her safari tent!" Ranger Gil continued.

More clapping.

"I guess that means I'm gonna win first place," Beatrice said to no one in particular as she admired her nails.

Joe rolled his eyes.

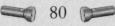 80

"And our first-place winner is Frank and Joe Hardy with their snake tent!" Ranger Gil said. "Boys, come up and get your trophy, and also your gift certificate for camping gear at Sal's Sporting Goods!"

The Hardys jumped to their feet. "Perry, Bob, and Andy delivered!" Joe said with a grin.

The brothers gave each other a high five.

Later, as Joe, Mr. Hardy, Phil, and Chet broke down their tents, Frank sat cross-legged on the ground with his notebook on his lap. The tip on his pencil was almost gone. He thought for a moment, then flipped to the page about their case.

He wrote:

WHO: ~~Lina?~~
~~Beatrice?~~
~~Garrett?~~
~~A person with the initials HOF?~~
Wendy!

WHY: ~~Maybe the person really wants~~
~~to win the tent-decorating contest?~~

~~Or maybe the person just wants to make trouble?~~

~~Or maybe it's just a bunch of stupid camp pranks?~~

Fish told Wendy that she should make things fun for the campers. She thought it would be cool if she made stuff disappear and reappear (like our snakes, Princess Petunia, and Mr. Truffles), and if she pretended to be a ghost.

Frank smiled to himself and added at the very end:

SECRET FILES CASE #16: SOLVED!

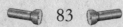

Join Zeus and his friends as they set off on the adventure of a lifetime.

Now Available:

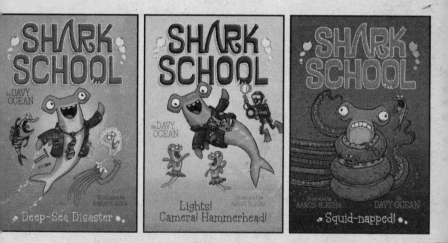

WHEN YOU'RE A KID, the MYSTERIES ARE JUST that MUCH *BIGGER* . . .

NANCY DREW AND THE CLUE CREW
SECRET SAND SLEUTHS

All-new comics from PAPERCUTZ!